Black Girl Sings the Blues

By Lola Blount

Black Girl Sings The Blues
Written by Lola Blount
2021 © Lola Blount
Published by: Empressed for Life Presents
Publishing Group LLC

Chapter 1
Bella's beginnings

"Ah, momma, it hurts."

"What's wrong, Precious?"

"I think my water broke, " Claire uttered
through the sharp contractions.

"Are you sure?"

"Yes, momma. I am sure."

"Okay, let me call the ambulance."

The ambulance came twenty minutes later.
The emergency medical technicians scooped
Claire up from the floor. She was writhing
in pain and felt as if her ass hole was about
to burst open.

Claire was rushed to Jacobi Hospital
accompanied by her mother, Symphony.
It wasn't even ten minutes after being
checked in did Claire deliver a baby girl.

The baby was whisked away. After
numerous attempts to question the doctor on

her baby's whereabouts, a stern-looking doctor entered to give the ladies an update.

"Ms. Claire Simpson, the baby weighed in at 4 pounds 11 ounces, and we also…."

"Bella, her name is Bella, " Claire interrupted the doctor.

"Um, fine, Bella weighed in at 4 pounds and 11 ounces. We also found heroin in her system. So we are going to keep her. Child protective services have also been called."

"What?" Claire and her mother asked in unison.

"Hospital policy when a baby is born addicted to a substance. Do you have any questions at all?"

Both women stared at the doctor with fire in their eyes. There wasn't any way they were willing to leave little Bella at the hospital. They didn't care what the hospital procedures were.

"Doctor, I'm Bella's grandmother. I'm also living in the home with Claire, and I'm not on any drugs. Why can't the baby be

released into my custody?" Symphony
asked.

"That's not up for us to decide. That
decision is best left up to the social workers.
Now, if that will be all, I have rounds to
attend to."

"Well, I guess that will be all, " Symphony
started sadly.

The doctor exited the room leaving the
ladies looking somber. Claire broke the
awkward silence first.
"Now what, momma?"

"Now you are asking for my advice? How
dare you?"

"Why are you upset with me?"

"Why am I upset with you? Is that a serious
question?"

"Yes, momma. It is. My whole life, you
have been unable to love me the way I
needed you to!"

"So you turn to drugs?"

"Yes!"

"And so you say I haven't been able to love you your whole life, yet you had a hot meal all your life, clean clothes, and a roof over your head. You may have been deprived of fancy name-brand items, but I worked two, sometimes three jobs to ensure you were taken care of. So please don't blame me for your choice to stick a needle in your arm and while pregnant, of all things. How dare you place the blame on me?"

Claire and Symphony each started crying. They were lost in their own thoughts. Suddenly a pair walked into the hospital room.

"Ms. Simpson, " the short, black, portly lady said.

"Yes, " Claire spoke up, terrified, knowing the duo represented the Department of Administration for Children's Services.

"I'm Mrs. Williams, and this is Mrs. Cornell. We are here to inform you that your daughter is now a ward of the state of New York unless her father comes forward and there isn't any evidence of drug use, we can investigate his home and place the child in his care."

"That will be impossible, " Claire cried out. "Momma, do something."

Symphony rolled her eyes at her daughter, then looked at Mrs. Williams and Cornell, giving a fake smile.

"Ladies, I'm Symphony Evans. Claire's mother and Bella's grandmother. I'm a hardworking woman without any history of drug use and will be more than capable of caring for my granddaughter and her needs."

"First, we have to investigate your home, and if all is well, I am sure the agency should have no problem placing her with you. Your daughter Claire can have supervised visits as long as she is complying with the stipulations, which will be set forth by a judge to be determined at a later date. You know Covid-19 restrictions and things of that nature has everything backlogged."

"Well, Claire resides in my home."

"That presents a problem."

"I don't have to reside with them. I can stay at a friend's house, " Claire said to her mother's dismay. She knew the friends Claire had, and they were all drug-addicted or prostituting.

"Does she have to move out?" Symphony asked for clarification.

"Yes, she does. Otherwise, there'd be no need for us to remove the child from her custody."

"Momma, please just take her. I can stay with Lisa for a while. She does have that extra room she has been trying to rent. I am sure if I get welfare to pay her some type of rent, she will allow me to stay there."

"I don't know, Claire, " Symphony said, conflicted. In her heart, she wanted her daughter to just go to rehab so that she could become stable enough to care for her child.

"What do you mean, you don't know? I don't want Bella going into the foster care system. She is your grandchild, for goodness sake."

"I'll do it."

"Great. I will call Lisa."

"But on one condition…that you go to rehab and not some friend's house, or you will never get better enough to care for Bella."

"Rehab?"

"That's a great idea, Ms. Simpson seeing as that will most likely be one of your stipulations to gaining custody of your child back. We can talk here with the hospital and see what services we can connect you with.!"

"Just great, " Claire said, not willing to yet give up her party girl life but feeling as if she had no other choice. She heard horror stories from her friends who were once in the system, and she didn't want Bella to experience that pain.

"As for you, Mrs. Evans, we will come to your home Monday. Please ensure you are home between the hours of 12 pm – 4 pm and that everyone present has a mask on. Now, if you can just write down your name, address, and best contact number, someone will contact you by Friday to confirm Monday's appointment."

Symphony did as instructed, her fingers shaking all the time. She couldn't believe that Claire got herself into this mess, had the nerve to blame her for her drug use, yet dared to wail out like a child for her help. If Bella weren't an innocent party in all of this, plus her granddaughter, she would have turned her back on Claire and told her to fend for herself the best way she knew how.

"So, will that be all?" Symphony asked the workers while throwing daggers at her eyes at Claire. She wanted to rip her head from her shoulders, but truth be known, she did have a part in Claire's lifestyle. She was an enabler.

"Yes, the baby has to remain in the hospital for further testing and until she gains the desired weight to be discharged. By then, your home should be inspected, and we should be able to have her placed with you directly from the hospital to your home. And Claire, we will work on coordinating with your doctors to get you situated for rehab."

"Thank you, " was all Claire and Symphony managed to say.

They watched as the two workers left the room. Then Symphony turned to Claire.

"And don't you ever say I couldn't love you the way you needed to be loved. I always come through for you when you need me. So don't ever disrespect me like that again."

"Oh, you want to go there, momma? How about when I told you your dirty-ass, alcoholic husband climbed into bed with me when I was only 11 years old? What did you tell me? Huh? And I quote, 'Now Claire, it's not nice to lie on people.'

"Your right. I didn't believe you then, and I don't believe you now. But besides all of that, I will be taking Bella, so god helps me if you don't follow my directions and those of the court. You've always been too fast for your good. Well, today, that shit stops."

"Momma?"

"Don't momma me. Once again, here I come to the rescue for someone who has harbored ill feelings for me. By the grace of God, Bella turns out better than her sorry ass excuse for a mother. Now I don't want to hear another word from you, young lady, until your ass is registered in rehab. I will find my grandbaby to sit with her for a few then go and get that house together. God only knows what junkie paraphernalia I will find in your room. "

With her head held high, Symphony made her academy-winning performance exit, never looking back to see how badly Claire was crying now. Not like she would have cared. Symphony blamed Claire for every misfortune in her life, but she was her child, so Symphony felt obligated to stick by her although her love was conditional. But this whole situation with Bella being born addicted to drugs and having to come live with her was the straw that broke Symphony's back. She would no longer coddle Claire out of obligations. This was spades, and she knew she had the winning hand to make Claire's life as miserable as Claire had done to her since the day she was born. And she intended to do just that.

Chapter 2
Bella's homecoming

Bella was released into Symphony's care under the kinship program a month after being taken from Claire's custody.

 Bella was still a ward of the state, but Symphony provided physical care for her. Symphony was to receive a small stipend to help with Bella's maintenance.

Claire was registered in an outpatient facility that combined psychological treatment with science-based techniques. While receiving her services, Claire resided with Lisa.

However, that situation was short-lived after Claire's first court date. She was ordered to go to a women's shelter so that she could find permanent housing so upon successful completion of her program, Bella could be returned to a stable environment.

The judge and agency workers agreed that a roommate situation wasn't a stable environment. Especially after making a surprise visit to check on Claire's progress, there were many young men with gang ties, weed-smoking, and drug paraphernalia lying around.

The agency workers recommended having Bella permanently removed from her mother's custody, citing her lack of ability to stop using drugs and partying.

Claire argued that she was not the legal tenant and only renting a room. Therefore she didn't have the right to mandate who was in and out of the residence.

The judge allowed her a bit of leniency but was firm on her going into the shelter.

At home, Symphony was in all her glory. She doted on Bella as if she were her child. Although she and her daughter had a strained relationship, she was happy that Bella was now in her care.

Symphony was now working from home, so there wasn't a need for a babysitter or daycare. Most days, she held Bella in her arms, talking to her ass if she could understand her.

Today was the day she had to take Bella to the agency on Waters street so that Claire could have her supervised visit.

As Symphony dressed the two of them, a dreadful feeling washed over her. Shaking it off, she proceeded to continue the task at hand.

She placed Bella in her baby seat then proceeded to go to her parking garage. Climbing into her red 2018 Honda Odyssey, she noticed her cell phone vibrating. It was Mrs. Williams.

"Hello, I'm on my way, " Symphony started in one breath.

"I guess you aren't aware of the circumstances."

"Circumstances?" Symphony asked out of confusion.

"Yes, your daughter is presently in Montefiore hospital due to an overdose. She started she was trying to kill herself when the shelter staff found her."

"Oh my goodness, why? I thought everything was fine with her. We just spoke yesterday via Facetime, " Symphony cried.

"That's something you will have to talk to her about. They gave her Narcan and pumped her stomach. Once they monitor her, she will be going to the psych ward on a mandatory hold."

"This just keeps getting worse, " Symphony thought to herself but still listened intently.

"So the reason for my call is, of course, to inform you that supervised visits have been canceled until we have a better idea of what is going on with Claire, her mental state, and release date."

"Of course, I understand."

"Also, we need to schedule another home visit."

"Of course, I understand. I want to go to the hospital to check on Claire, but if you are coming now, I can wait."

"Yes, I will be there within the hour or so."

"Sure, Mrs. Williams, see you then."

Symphony got out of the car and retrieved the car seat with little Bella in it, then headed back to her home, crying all the way there.

Her neighbor Mr. Bixby tried to say good morning to her as was his custom, but she waved him off.

Sensing something was wrong, he tried to get her to confide in him.

"You know it might help to talk about things. Maybe we can find a solution to what bothers you."

"There's no solution for this since I'm not the one with the issue, " she remarked snidely. "Now, good day to you, sir."

Symphony hastened her steps, not wanting to be the victim to his lustful glances. He was fine. She had to admit that, but his timing was off, way off.

Making it home and getting Bella into more comfortable attire, she waited anxiously for Mrs. Williams to arrive. When she did, it seemed there was a chip on her shoulder.

After checking the dresser draws, bedrooms, and food cabinets to ensure Bella had enough formula, diapers, and baby clothes, she turned to Symphony.

"My job isn't to play games by lying to you. I have seen cases such as Claire's before, and a person like that never gets clean no matter how many chances they are given. As a result, on the next court date, I am seriously asking the judge to be firm and terminate Claire's parental rights."

"While I may understand your position, I am not in full agreement. God can take the worst of people and turn them into saints. Please don't be so quick to make this request. I am sure she can pull it together."

"My mind is made up, and I was hoping to have you on board with this. You have a nice home, and it would be a shame to remove Bella from here, but I will."

"I heard of playing hardball, but your statement sounds more like a threat. Are you threatening me?"

"No, I'm not making any threats. I am just making my position clear, " Mrs. Williams stated.

"Understood, and you can make all the recommendations in the world, but I will spend my life savings fighting you in court for custody of my grandchild. Now my daughter may not be level-headed and stable, but I damn sure am. Good day, Mrs. Williams. I believe we are done here, " Symphony started, then stormed to the door and opened it for Mrs. Williams to leave.

"Good day Mrs. Evans. You will be hearing from me again."

"And I am sure the pleasure will be all mine."

Symphony closed the door harshly then went to grab her favorite brand of red wine from her antique wine cabinet. She poured herself a tall glass and went on the patio to drink her wine and smoke a cigar while Bella napped. She couldn't believe Mrs. Williams, but more than that, she couldn't believe Claire and the position she had put them all in.

Symphony knew she had to check on Claire to find out for herself what was going on, but there wasn't any way she could ain't beside her and not wrap her hands around her neck. As a result, she decided to call the hospital for an update only to find out Claire went awol. She left the hospital against doctors ' orders.

Bewildered as to what was going on with her child, she now realizes the uphill battle she would have on her hands with not only Mrs. Williams but Claire.

Symphony took the last large gulp of wine in her glass and poured another one. She couldn't believe her luck, but at least Bella was safe.

"I'll kill her, " Symphony uttered through clenched teeth regarding Claire. She meant every word too. It was simply a matter of time.

Chapter 3

Finding Claire

After gathering her thoughts, Symphony checked her phone's contacts for Claire's friends' numbers.

She called Lisa first, who said she hadn't heard from Claire but to try Geia.

Geia was a close teenage friend of Claire's. They met in high school.

Like Claire, Geia also had a history of drug addiction. Symphony silently hoped that Claire wasn't with Geia. Indulging in drugs should be Claire's last resort considering her condition.

Symphony also wondered why Claire wouldn't want to get her life together for Bella, who didn't ask to be in this world. Claire decided to birth her. Now Claire should step up to the plate and do whatever it takes to raise her. Bella should not be her responsibility, but she was her grandchild. As a result, Symphony was willing to be the one to shoulder the responsibility.

Symphony dressed Bella once more to run an errand at the grocery store. She needed some green peppers and plantains to accompany her oxtails and jasmine rice.

Instead of driving, Symphony placed Bella in her Fendi stroller and walked. She felt as if the cool air would help clear her head of the racing thoughts.

Mr. Bixby was still outside tending to his rose bushes. He glanced at Claire but decided against speaking. He could tell she was still in an irritable mood and decided to speak with her when she was in a better state of mind.

Symphony was grateful he didn't speak as she didn't want to be rude. She briskly walked to the grocery store, paid for her items, and headed back home when she spotted a familiar person.

As she got closer to the image, their features came into view. It was Claire. She was nodding off in an apparent drug stupor.

Using her cell phone, Symphony placed a call to 911. She relayed the gravity of the situation and gave their exact location. When Emergency Medical technicians arrived, they placed Claire onto a gurney.

Symphony folded the stroller with one hand and held the baby in the other. They accompanied Claire to the hospital, where she was readmitted for drug use.

Symphony requested for Claire to be placed in a rehabilitation center. After waiting some time, she spoke to a social worker that informed her after Claire's assessment. They would make the necessary recommendations.

Symphony could do nothing else but go home and wait for the social worker's phone call.

Symphony went home to watch television. She loved reality series. The women on those shows cut up something terrible, providing an escape from the issues of her very own reality.

She placed baby Bella in her crib. She washed her hands and prepped her dinner. Afterward, Symphony poured another glass of wine then settled down to relax for a moment.

Once dinner finished cooking, she ate, gave
Bella her bath, and showered. She fell into
an uneasy sleep with dreams of Claire.

In these dreams, Claire overdosed and died.
Symphony woke up in a cold sweat. She
raced to the bathroom and threw cold water
on her face.

Sitting back in bed, she turned on her gospel
low and let the music console her broken
heart and weary mind.

This time she drifted off to sleep without
any disturbances until Bella woke up. She
fed her, staring into her almond-shaped eyes.

Symphony wasn't an overly religious
woman, but she did not lack faith. She
prayed over her grandchild, asking for God's
guidance to raise her the right way.

Current times seemed worse than when she
was raising Claire. The availability to obtain
drugs was at an all-time high.

Modern-day technology made drugs seem cool and education or employment for fools.

To raise Bella, there had to be a better way. She was going to find it, come hell or high waters.

Chapter 4

Sometimes all you need is a friend

Symphony wasn't able to wait for the social worker to contact her regarding Claire's condition. As a result, she placed a call to the social worker only to be greeted by a voicemail stating the mailbox was full and couldn't accept any more messages.

She revealed the number numerous times to no avail. Feeling as if she didn't have any other choice, she called the social worker's supervisor.

Thankfully she was able to reach her. Ms. George, the supervisor, stated that Mrs. Acevedo was in the field working with other client's and she would be sure to have the social worker give Symphony a call as soon as she returned.

Symphony thanked her, but in her heart, she wanted to rant and rave. She didn't understand what took so long to give an assessment. Weren't client's in Claire's position a priority?

As if the day couldn't get any worse, she received a call from Mrs. Williams, who wanted to make another home visit.

Symphony wasn't a fool. She knew Mrs. Williams's interest wasn't only to check on Bella and play hardball with her to strip Claire of her parental rights.

Although Claire was horrible, Symphony did not like the games she felt Mrs. Williams was playing.

"But you just visited Mrs. Williams. I can assure you that Bella is fine. I am taking very good care of my grandchild."

"While that may be true, I still have to make visits to ensure Bella is being taken care of. I can not just take your word for it. Plus, the last visit wasn't too pleasant."

"Gee, you think?" Symphony started sarcastically, rolling her eyes as she did.

"I'm sorry. Repeat that, " Mrs. Williams requested sternly.

"Nothing, " Symphony caved in, knowing that Mrs. Williams held her grandchild's fate in her hands. The last thing Symphony wanted was to battle it out with Mrs. Williams because of a few tricky words.

"Listen, Mrs. Williams, I understand you have a job to do, and I am not trying to get in the way of that. All I want to do is take care of my grandchild, and I owe her that much. Bella did not ask to be born to a drug-addicted mother. But the past few months have been challenging. Given your line of work, I am sure you can understand."

"Yes, all too well. Now when will be a good time for you. Mrs. Cornell and I can be there in a few hours."

"I'm sorry. Did you say a few hours?" Symphony asked, stalling because she desperately wanted a report regarding Claire, so she knew how to approach Mrs. Williams and Mrs. Cornell's visit.

"Yes, a few hours. Mrs. Cornell and I have to submit our report to the agency by the week's end and have a few more things I need to go over with you."

"Is it possible for you to come tomorrow by noon? I have a doctor's appointment today but will definitely be home tomorrow, ” Symphony lied, hoping to gain more time to speak with the social worker. She needed to know about Claire's condition and if the hospital recommended Claire to a rehab center.

“Sure. Mrs. Cornell and I will see you tomorrow at noon. Good day, ” Mrs. Williams stated, then hung up without waiting for an answer.

Symphony stared at her phone in skepticism. “This can not be life, ” she uttered.

Symphony wanted to crawl into bed and cry all day, but she had a zoom meeting with a client.

Symphony changed her attire and put on a pink dress shirt and slacks. She remained barefoot, knowing the camera wouldn't be able to peer in that low.

On her head, Symphony wore a baby pink headwrap with black designs. She applied a bit of gloss to her lips and made sure her lashes were on straight.

The meeting went well, and she was able to snag a new client for her business venture. She loved working from home.

Then reality set in when Mrs. Acevedo returned her call. Although it seemed like an eternity, the call was promising.

It was at least something positive to report to Mrs. Cornell and Mrs. Williams, seeing as that Claire would be sent to a rehab clinic within the next few days.

After 28 days, Claire would either be released or recommended for further treatment.

Symphony thanked Mrs. Acevedo for returning her call with an update.

Instead of giving in to the temptation to lay around in bed for the rest of the day, she remained in her work clothes, had a quick glass of red wine, then dressed Bella to go on a stroll.

Once outside, she ran into Mr. Bixby again. Symphony apologized for her behavior the other day, and before one knew it, her tears were flowing. She explained to Mr. Bixby all that had been occurring with Claire and Bella.

Me. Bixby gave Symphony a caress on the back and assumed her he understood.

"Listen, I am here for you to vent to when times become rough. There's a no-judgment zone with me. I've done traveled many paths in life, encountered many people that were into many things. Plus, I am not God. I am God-fearing but not God. Trust, you will always have a friend to vent to and a shoulder to lean on during good or bad times, " Mr. Bixby declared.

"I am so glad to hear that, " Symphony said, relieved.

"Hey, do you drink?"

"Just wine, " Symphony responded.

"Cool. Why don't you and the baby come in for a while? We will put on some smooth tunes, have a sip of wine, and take your mind off your problems."

"Sure, I don't see why not, " Symphony said, then followed closely behind Mr. Bixby into his home, thinking to herself that sometimes all you need is a friend.

Chapter 5

Symphony Gets Her Groove
Back…Almost

Once inside Mr. Bixby's home, Symphony had to admit it was amazing.

He had cream-white vintage furniture with coffee tables to match. It was very nostalgic and reminded her of youthful days spent in the times of her elders.

He did add a bit of modernized furniture in the form of a 50-inch television.

Baby Bella had drifted into a peaceful sleep in her stroller.

Mr. Bixby poured two glasses of wine plus shots of tequila on the side.

He turned on an old school jam by The Delfonics, and the two began to talk more in-depth about Symphony and Claire's problems. Mr. Bixby suggested tough love as a course of remedy.

He also suggested from now on; Symphony recorded conversations between herself and the ACS workers.

The pair had a few more glasses of wine minus the tequila shots.

Within the next hour or so, the wine Mr. Bixby and Symphony drunk had them feeling nice and mellow. The pair began to slow dance.

It had been a while since Symphony was in the company of a man, let alone in their arms. It felt nice and was enticing.

Then Mr. Bixby placed a soft passionate kiss on Symphony's lips. She pulled back. She liked the kiss but was startled at the suddenness of it all.

"I'm sorry. Is something wrong? Did I pass my place?" he asked, gently staring into her eyes.

Symphony hesitated. She was thinking of the right words to say without being offensive.

The awkward moments of silence led him to release her.

"I'm sorry it won't happen again, " Mr. Bixby stated warmly.

"No, the kiss was nice. It was just so unexpected, and it had been so long since any man has touched me in such a sensual manner."

"Oh my, I really feel bad now."

"Why?"

"Because I never want to put a rush on a woman who may not be ready for the level of intimacy that I may want."

"I understand, " Symphony started. Thought to herself for a minute, then continued, "but the kiss was nice. So I don't feel rushed, I don't feel overwhelmed, and I damn sure don't think you passed your place."

"Whew, I don't ever want to hurt you. So would you like to end our little soiree?"

"No, one more glass of wine and dance would be fine with me. How about you?"

"Sound like a plan," Mr. Bixby happily agreed.

Needless to say, the pair had two more glasses of wine. They even danced some more. Yet this time, it was Symphony who leaned in for a kiss.

Mr. Bixby's hands immediately caressed her soft breast. She let out a whimper of lust.

He continued caressing her. Symphony almost melted into his arms. Their kisses became more passionate.

Mr. Bixby started to undress Symphony when Bella woke up crying.

"Go ahead and tend to the baby. She comes first, " Mr. Bixby said.

"Thank you, " was all Symphony could manage as she tried to get her bearings about her.

Once her clothes were neat and her feelings gathered, she picked up the baby, realizing Bella needed her diaper changed.

"Let me take her home and bathe her. I had such a lovely time, but like you said, she comes first."

"Yes, and I wasn't lying. We can do this again. Have another-soiree. That is if you don't mind."

"No, I don't mind at all. In fact, I look forward to it, "Symphony admitted.

"Great. How about next week Friday? I will even cook for you. What is your favorite dish?"

"Gee, a dinner too? You are so kind. I might get spoiled, "Symphony said teasingly.

"You deserve to be spoiled, " he said admiringly.

"To be honest, there are so many, but if I had to pick, it would be anything soul food or anything Italian."

"Great, I know just what to make for you. Let me walk you home."

The pair and baby Bella left the house. The air was cool and crisp, so he put his arm around Symphony. She enjoyed his scent.

Once at her door, he gave her a light peck on the lips. Then they said their goodbyes.

Symphony went inside, turned on her Debarge playlist on iTunes, bathed, and fed Bella.

Once Bella's needs were taken care of, Symphony made herself a spinach salad with grilled chicken and vinaigrette dressing.

Baby cartoons were on the television while she ate, and Bella cooed.

Once Symphony's stomach was satisfied, Bellas attention occupied, she took a quick shower. Then put on her pajamas and placed Bella in her crib.

Symphony climbed into her own bed and snuggled under the covers. That night there weren't any crazy dreams, just a well-needed rest.

But upon waking, all hell was breaking out with Claire and the hospital.

"If it's not one thing, it's another Symphony said out loud before reciting the Serenity Prayer.

Chapter 6

Fight the Powers that be

Once Symphony reached the hospital, after taking Bella to the daycare center on White Plains Road, Claire was sedated. The hospital staff decided not to press charges even though Claire was out of control.

Claire assaulted hospital staff. One nurse was left with a black and blue mark on her rosy-colored face.

The administrator in charge said Claire refused to take her medication. Upon instance, by staff, Claire had a violent outburst.

Symphony was in tears watching her child act a tool. She wondered why Claire couldn't get her life and emotions together.

While Symphony felt Claire was young enough to have a bright future, Claire would sabotage that if she didn't focus on her rehabilitation.

At this point, Symphony felt prayer and divine intervention would be the only thing things that would help Claire adjust and live a semblance of a normal life.

This was necessary so that Bella would have a chance to live a healthy life with a loving parent.

The administrator allowed Symphony to have a moment with Claire. She went to her gurney, gently placing her hand on Claire's head. She was feverish.

Symphony looked around and found the nurse's call button. She asked for a cool rag. After they brought Symphony the rag, she placed it on Claire's forehead and kissed her on the cheek.

She then held Claire's hands in her own and said a silent prayer to God. Symphony asked her to heal Claire of her afflictions.

Symphony held onto Claire's hands for dear life, willing to her to fight the inner demons she must have been battling.

After fifteen minutes of praying and holding onto Claire, a stocky-built nurse informed Symphony it was time to go.

"Mommy loves you and will be back. You are strong enough to get through this," Symphony said to a worn-out Claire.

Claire opened her eyes and gave a weary smile.

"I love you too, mommy," Claire responded, giving Symphony a glimmer of hope that the child she raised would become whole again.

Symphony raced to the daycare to get Bella. After the experience she had with Claire, the only thing in the world she wanted to do was hold the purest part Claire brought into the world, her baby girl.

Symphony rushed through the daycare doors without greeting anyone and headed straight towards Bella, but something seemed off.

Bella had a bruise under her eye.

"What happened here," Symphony admonished.

"Ma'am, we are sorry, but a child hit Bella by accident."

"Accident? In her face? You've got to be shitting me," Symphony started, not believing the luck her family encountered lately.

"Yes, Ma'am. A new enrollment became excited when seeing Bella and went to kiss her. However, the buckle of her knapsack caught Bella in the eye. The nurse iced it, but it left a slight bruise."

"I want to see the videotape. I see the cameras, so don't lie."

"Hold on, let me ask the owner."

"Hold on? Ask the owner? What type of establishment is this?" Symphony yelled dramatically, causing a scene.

"I got it, Miriam," the owner Tiffany stated. She was red in complexion with a short pixie haircut and deep freckles on her face.

"And you are?"

"Tiffany Clarke, the owner and manager, Ms. Evans, and I need to ask you to calm down. Let's not excite the children."

"Well, if you and your staff kept a closer eye on the children, my granddaughter wouldn't have a bruise on her face, now would she?"

"I understand your frustration. Follow me. I will show you the tape," Ms. Clarke stated, handling the situation as best as she could without losing her professionalism.

Symphony picked up Bella and held her tightly, planting sweet kisses to the top of her forehead.

The trio went into Ms. Clarke's office, where they viewed the tape.

The incident happened the way the teacher said it did. All Symphony could do was apologize.

After leaving the daycare, Symphony cried. She cried out of frustration over Claire's condition, cried over the embarrassment of going to the extreme at the daycare center. Most of all, Symphony cried because she was heartbroken. Her family was in shambles, and she didn't know how to fix it, but she was going to do her best or die trying.

Chapter 7

Safe in his arms

The next day Symphony completed her work tasks, tended to Bella, received an update from the hospital regarding Claire. Then went for a stroll. She hesitated when she reached Mr. Bixby's house. Symphony wanted to see him badly. She needed friendly adult conversation—someone who could look at her family's situation through a neutral lens.

Symphony knocked lightly on the door. She was nervous that she popped up. What if he was in the midst of entertaining another woman, working, or just didn't want to be bothered by her presence.

To her delight, none of her fears were realized. Mr. Bixby was more than happy to see her. He invited her in. After sitting, he engaged her in conversation.

"So what brings you by here?" he asked, showing his pearly whites.

"Should I have not come by? I mean, I don't want to be rude or obnoxious or anything."

"You aren't any of those things. I am pleasantly surprised. I was cooking when you knocked. Would you like a plate?"

"It depends on what you made."

" Grilled shrimp with a spinach salad topped with feta cheese, and I have vinaigrette and ranch dressing for starters."

"For starters? You mean there is more?"

"Yes, I have roasted red onions and peppers with fettuccine with Alfredo sauce and calamari. "

"Dang, don't think I am greedy but give me all of that!"

The pair broke out into a fit of laughter.

"Follow me," he said softly.

They went into the kitchen where Mr. Bixby fixed Symphony a plate containing the hefty meal. He pulled a bottle of red wine from the cabinet and poured two glasses.

He sat down across from Symphony, smiling.

"What you aren't eating with me?" she asked, puzzled.

"I already ate. So in the meantime, I just want to sit here and watch you eat my creation. You sure are a work of art, so I don't mind."

"Me a work of art? I look a hot mess," Symphony giggled uneasily, anxiously patting her hair.

"You're a beautiful hot mess, and I can't wait to hold you."

"Hold me?" she repeated breathlessly, remembering their close encounter during her last visit.

"Yes, eat up. I love the scenery."

Symphony decided to loosen up a bit. She took another bite of her food while training her eyes on Mr. Bixby. He was handsome indeed, and suddenly the thoughts of him holding her and other sexual things didn't seem too scary.

After Symphony ate and the pair had three glasses of wine, Mr. Bixby held and fed baby Bella. He even put her to sleep.

Once Bella was tucked away safely sleeping, he turned the volume to the radio on low. Soft rhythm and blues permeated the room.

He grabbed Symphony, and the two began to slow dance. After a few tender moments, he held her at arm's length and undressed her with his eyes. He pulled her in close to him and whispered a few sensual words in her ear, and then he began to undress her truly.

Symphony matched his intensity, and the two undressed each other. Naked, they stood as the day they were born admiring each other's bodies.

Mr. Bixby began caressing Symphony. She allowed him to hold her breath as he reached her golden spot. She gasped.

"Are you okay?"

"Yes, please continue."

He spread her legs apart, placed one on his shoulder then licked her sweet nectar. She orgasmed instantly, trying to push his head from her inner parts.

"Am I hurting you?"

"No, the heat. Wow, it's been so long."

"Relax, lay down on the floor," he instructed, guiding her down. He propped her head on cushions then went back to his task at hand.

Symphony orgasmed several times. Her legs were a quivering mess. Afterward, she lay spent and safe in his arms, nuzzled in the fur of his chest, forgetting her troubles with Claire. It was the most beautiful moment she remembered sharing with anyone, but as expected, in her world, all good things end.

Chapter 8

Six months later

Claire's return

To everyone's amazement, Claire successfully completed her rehabilitation program. She was transferred to a single woman's shelter and was mandated by the courts to attend Narcotics anonymous.

After a three-month suspension of her supervised visits with Bella to monitor her progress, the visits were allowed at Symphony's home.

Some nights when Symphony thought it was safe, she would allow Claire to spend the night. Symphony usually allowed this once Mrs. Williams conducted her home visits. They almost were caught a few times, but Mrs. Williams overlooked it. It seemed as if Mrs. Williams was having a change of heart because she updated Claire and Bella's status as a return to the parent. Mrs.

Williams was hoping it would take a year or less. Claire would still have home visits conducted by Mrs. Williams and her colleagues, but Claire would still have primary parental custody over Bella, and that's what mattered most of all.

While Claire was dressing baby Bella in her Easter outfit, Symphony decided to talk with her to see where Claire's head was really at.

"I know you are taking parenting classes, going to outpatient rehab, and complying with the shelter rules, but what are you doing about school or employment?"

"Ma, I am just so consumed, I haven't had time to think about it."

"Well, you need to start thinking because when you are granted permanent custodial partnership over your child, how will you feed her?"

"I haven't thought that far ahead yet," Claire admitted.

"Well, you better start thinking because the time will be here before we both realize it."

The doorbell rang, and to Symphony's surprise, it was Mr. Bixby. She instantly became excited and let him in.

" Well, hi, you must be Claire. I'm.."

"I know who you are… The creepy guy from down the block who is always starting at everybody."

"Claire, mind your manners," Symphony said, embarrassed. "Bixby is a dear friend of mine."

"Bixby, huh? Even your name is weird," Claire continued with being disrespectful.

"Claire, I won't tell you again to mind your manners in front of my company. If I have to, I will put your ass out. Now, do you understand me?"

There was an awkward silence as Claire pursed her lips in an attempt not to respond.

"I said, do you understand me?"

Me. Bixby was visibly shaken but tried to brush it off.

"It's alright, Symphony. Maybe I should have called first."

"Maybe you should have," Claire retorted.

"That's it, young lady. You have to leave now. Pass me, Bella."

"No!" Claire shouted.

"You have made enough of a scene. I said, pass me, Bella, now before I smack the holy shit out of you," Symphony said, losing her self-control.

"Ma, you mean to tell me you are putting me out for this creep?" Claire asked, astounded.

"If my visiting is causing so much drama, I will just leave."

"No, my daughter knows how to mind her business and her manners. I welcome you in my home, and if she has a problem with a visitor of mine, she can just leave," Symphony declared boldly.

"I ain't got to go anywhere. Call the police if you want me out."

Symphony had enough of Claire and her drama. Symphony walked straight to where Claire was standing, then hauled off and smacked the shit out of her.

The whole room was stunned, even Symphony, who lost control of her faculties. She was about to hit Claire again, forgetting that Claire was holding Bella until Mr. Bixby intervened.

"That's enough, Symphony. I'm sorry that my presence is such a disturbance for you; I can assure you I am not a creep. In fact, I love both your mother and child very much. One day I hope even to marry Symphony.

Symphony was shocked at Mr. Bixby's announcement, and so was Claire. However, Claire's shock was more of disappointment. She couldn't understand why as young and pretty as she was, it would be her mother to marry first.

"Oh, you want to marry my mother, but the way you look at me, it's as if you want to fuck me!" Claire said, dying to get that off her chest.

"Whaaat?" Symphony and Bixby exclaimed in unison.

"You heard me, ma! Your dude here wants to fuck me!"

"I can assure you, Symphony, that's not the case. I am friendly with all neighbors, lived in this area since my youthful days, and besides my first wife who transitioned from cancer, you are the only other woman I have dated or been intimate with."

"I believe you, honey. Claire has been doing this since she was a child. Every time I am happy, she tries to ruin it with some concocted story. Well, this one I am not going for."

Symphony turned to Claire and snatched Bella out of her arms. She marched to the door and opened it quickly.

"Claire, you can leave now and don't come back until you remember your manners and how to show respect to my future husband because it's no longer all about you. I found a man who says he wants to marry me one day, and I am willing to marry him."

Claire looked at Mr. Bixby, then her mother. Tears formed in her eyes, and she left silently vowing to exact revenge, not only on Mr. Bixby for ruining her relationship with her mother but also revenge on her mother for choosing yet another man over her.

'They will regret this,' Claire thought to herself as she stormed to the train station to return to her room at the dreary single women's shelter.

Chapter 9

Comforted

"I'm sorry about that, Bixby," Symphony apologetically stated.

"No, need. I am a pretty understanding guy, and I understand Claire has her issues. Just know I don't want to be the reason you don't have a relationship with your daughter."

"No, my daughter would be the reason I don't have a relationship with my daughter. Sad as it may be, I am becoming used to her antics. I'm just sorry you got caught up in the mix of things."

"Don't be sorry. Come here, let me give you a big hug. I know your nerves are frazzled now."

"They sure are, and a hug sounds delightful and useful."

The couple embraced, and she melted into his strong arms. Safe and comforted are what she felt—also enveloped by his love. The pair had been dating for six months now, and Symphony felt as if she couldn't live without him visiting to ensure she and Bella were alright. The feelings she carried for Bixby were both exciting and eerie.

Symphony tried not to think negative thoughts regarding their relationship not working. Truth be known, she had been hurt so many times in the past it made her a pessimist. To feel such love from Bixby was somewhat unnatural. Although she didn't doubt that he loved her, she doubted things might end terribly between the two of them. Symphony couldn't help but think Claire would be the reason. Especially after Claire's actions tonight.

After embracing for a while, Symphony went into the kitchen to cook for her man. She made eggplant parmesan with Zeppole's and garlic bread. The pair are in silence until Bella let it be known she wanted out of her playpen.

Symphony tended to her while Bixby cleared the table and washed the dishes. He even scrubbed the pots.

Symphony loved having Bixby around. He was so helpful. He lightened her load and was a light in her and Bella's life.

Now, if only she could do the same with Claire. Before the two had a chance to catch their breath after cleaning, an unexpected knock came.

Thinking it was Claire, Symphony flung open the door.

"And what do you want?" but to Symphony's surprise and dismay, it was Mrs. Williams.

"I'm sorry, did I catch you at a bad time. Claire called and said it was an emergency that we get over here," she said, pointing to her partner.

"That bitch," Symphony mumbled.

"I'm sorry, what?" Mrs. Williams asserted

Symphony invited Mrs. Williams inside, introduced her to Bixby and explained the situation.

Mrs. Williams said she understood but had to see how her supervisor wanted to deal with the matter.

After Mrs. Williams spoke with Bixby and jotted down his information such as name, address, and occupation; she decided not to remove Bella from Symphony's care but started she would be back.

Bixby and Symphony figured that much, and after Mrs. Williams left with her colleague, the two discussed the matter.

"What are you thinking?" Symphony asked Bixby.

"That my unannounced presence has placed you in a horrible position BUT if we are to get married we will live under the same roof. Meaning Claire is going to have to come to terms with me being around occupying your time. She can't be the spoiled brat that she is. Claire has to grow up or she will never be able to take care of Bella's emotional needs.

"I agree. I just know if that is possible when it comes to her. The drugs seem to have her mind clouded."

"I know, but with continuous rehab and counseling, we should start to see an improvement."

"Goodness, I hope so."

"Please be comforted by my words. In the not-so-far past, a family member went

through something similar. Today they are
an outstanding member of society.”

“I believe and trust you. You just don’t
know how much having you here has helped
me. Would you please hold me? I want to
feel your arms around me. They are so safe.”

Bixby held onto Symphony with all his
might. They even drifted off into a light
sleep until another knock came, and this
time, all the pair heard was, “Momma please
open the door. It’s me.”

Chapter 10

It's Drama Time

Claire

Claire was in such a state leaving her mother's house that she did the one thing she knew that she was good at…Got high.

Claire was still high as a kite when she arrived back her mother's house that she did the unthinkable.

Claire tried to take Bella from her mother. Symphony wasn't in the mood to play with Claire by catering to her feelings, especially with the state Claire was in.

Symphony politely placed Bella in her high chair out of Claire's grasp and commenced to fighting Claire.

It was a close fight, but Symphony got the best of Claire. Claire was defeated. Claire was also embarrassed.

The truth was Mr. Bixby never tried to make sexual advances towards Claire. Claire was just jealous Symphony had someone who loved her and Bella and wanted to interrupt that connection.

Claire never figured in the factor that it may not work. She was just hellbent on having her mother's undivided attention so Claire could have Symphony at her beck and call.

Claire also wanted some sort of payback for her upbringing and the childhood trauma Claire endured by the hands of Symphony's ex. Claire felt Symphony didn't handle the situation properly. For that, she wanted Symphony to pay even though Symphony was the only one in her corner.

Symphony stormed to the door to throw Claire out of her home while Mr. Bixby looked on in horror. He was shocked that his presence caused the two ladies to become entangled in a physical altercation but there wasn't anything he could do about it.

"Momma, please don't put me out. I still want to spend time with Bella."

"Not in my house. I am making sure you can only see her at the agency. You do not have the luxury of just popping up at my home anymore. Do you understand me Claire?"

Claire remained silent. Although she wanted to lash back out at her mother she knew it was best by the look on Symphony's face to not push her luck.

Claire looked pleadingly at Mr. Bixby who held up his hands as if to say, "I don't want any parts of this nonsense because you did it to yourself."

Claire even looked at Bella as if they baby could help. Coming to the realization she didn't have any allies in Symphony's house she exited the front door with her head hung low and tears streaming from her eyes.

Claire now sobered up and realized what a horrible mistake she made battling Symphony.

After Claire left, Symphony turned and ran to Mr. Bixby, who held her in his arms, embracing her tightly.

"It seems this is becoming our norm."

"No worries, my love. This too shall pass."

"I hope you are right, Bixby. I hope you are right."

Meanwhile, Claire was outside looking for a fix. She found a willing partner to buy her some drugs of her choice after telling them her version of events.

The buddy and Claire drove to a secluded parking area near Pelham Bay Park in the Bronx. There the two got as high as they could until passing out with the motor of the car still on and the radio full blast.

It was hours before a concerned citizen called the cops to come to perform a welfare check on the ladies.

The cops banged on the windows of the car, but only Claire came to her senses.

"Open the door ma'am," the round stern face cop with piercing blues eyes demanded.

Instead of opening the door, Claire rolled down the window and spoke.

"Problem officer?"

"Do you have identification, ma'am"

Claire informed the officer she did not have identification. She was then instructed to step out of the black 2000 Cutlass Sierra.

Claire was searched then handcuffed after the cop found two bags of heroin in her possession. At the same time his partner said, "Gotta get a stretcher for this one. She's blue and I can't find a pulse."

"Damn," was all Claire and the cop who handcuffed her could manage to say.

Chapter 11

The End

Claire couldn't believe the day she had. She physically fought with her mother and was put out of the house. She also got arrested but the worse part was knowing her friend was dead. There was nothing Claire could do to bring them back.

The judge wasn't lenient on her and denied her request of being released on her own recognizance. Instead, he set her bail at three thousand dollars due to the loss of life.

Symphony heard Claire's voice and then the phone hung up. Symphony refused to assist Claire and all Claire wanted to do was go home and get high. She needed to take the pain away. Claire didn't have the connections to do that from behind bars. As a result, she went to a corner of the cell and cried.

Claire would be transferred to the women's section on Riker's Island until she could either make bail or have a trial, whichever came first.

Claire tried numerous times to reach out to Symphony, but her efforts were in vain. Symphony refused to speak to Claire.

Symphony was fed up with her daughter. Symphony also felt since drug rehab didn't help Claire in getting her life together that maybe jail time was the answer.

Therefore Symphony wouldn't help Claire obtain legal counsel not would she pay the bail for her to be released.

Claire would simply have to lay in the bed she made for herself.

As for Symphony, she spent her time taking care of Bella, working, and in the company of Mr. Bixby. Things were going well for the couple. He even bought Symphony an engagement ring. Symphony couldn't be happier.

The next step for the pair was moving in together. They decided upon getting a new house so both of their names could go on the deed.

The new house was located in Riverdale in the Bronx. It was a quaint Victorian style, one-unit, two-story house. It had four bedrooms with two and a half bathrooms.

Symphony was in awe. The area was nice, and the daycare centers she visited to research for Bella were clean with rave reviews.

Symphony and Bixby decided to turn their former residences into Air BnBs. Being a new blended family household the extra streams of income would do a world of good. Plus, they also wanted to travel to not only different parts of the world but also internationally. The Bahamas would be their first trip as well as their honeymoon.

Seeing as the two didn't have many friends, they opted to get married at the courthouse and have a small gathering in the new house afterward.

The wedding day approached, and Symphony was a ball of nerves. It seemed Claire called her throughout the week over one hundred times, but she was standing firm on not speaking to Claire.

Symphony's dress was gorgeous. It was a cream-colored, body-hugging, lace Vera Wang dress. Bixby was dressed in a white silk suit with a navy-blue shirt, white bow tie, white brim hat, sterling silver cufflinks, and blue wing-tipped Stacy Adams with a silver swirled in them. Baby Bella wore an all cream down to her old-fashioned Mary Jane patent leather shoes. On her head was a beautiful bonnet and a basket with blue roses was her accessory.

Symphony put her phone on silent. She didn't want to be interrupted by Claire's foolishness. Today was Symphony's day, and nothing could destroy it.

The reception after the nuptials was just as beautiful. The food was catered by Gourmet Catering and Desserts. The wedding cake was three-tier chocolate with buttercream frosting and a black bride and groom on top.

After everyone partied and left, Symphony received a call from an unrecognizable number. Against Bixby's advice she answered. It was Claire crying that she had received a three-year sentence eligible for parole after 26 months.

"As I told you before you made your bed now lie in it, but this time do something with yourself like attend a class. Take your recovery serious and when you come home maybe I will take you seriously," Symphony started and thing up without waiting for Claire's response.

"Three years?" Bixby asked.

"Yes, three years of peace. Thank goodness the courts gave me permanent guardianship over Bella. Who knows what type of life she would have with Claire. She is my daughter, and I love her, but Claire has a lot of healing to do. I can't do it for her."

With that said, Symphony hugged her husband, and they danced to imaginary music only their heartbeats could hear. Symphony was in love, and that was all that mattered. She tried her best with Claire. Now it was up to Claire to fight her demons.

9 798791 024848